For my one and only "Big Kid" Amy . . .
an amazing artist and awesome daughter
All my love, Mom
&
To Doris and Larry . . .
for always being in my life, with your unconditional
and treasured love
Love, Debbie

For Stewart and Franklin, bunk bed brothers
—T.M.

Text copyright © 2017 by Debbie Bertram
Jacket art and interior illustrations copyright © 2017 by Taia Morley
All rights reserved. Published in the United States
by Random House Children's Books, a division of Penguin Random House LLC, New York.

Random House and the colophon are registered trademarks of Penguin Random House LLC.

Visit us on the Web! randomhousekids.com

Educators and librarians, for a variety of teaching tools,
visit us at RHTeachersLibrarians.com

Library of Congress Cataloging-in-Publication Data
Names: Bertram, Debbie, author. | Morley, Taia, illustrator.
Title: My new big-kid bed / Debbie Bertram, Taia Morley.
Description: First edition. | New York : Random House, [2017] | Summary: When his new dinosaur-themed bed
casts scary shadows at night, a child seeks comfort from other family members.
Identifiers: LCCN 2015043686 (print) | LCCN 2016020400 (ebook) |
ISBN 978-1-101-93731-0 (hardcover) | ISBN 978-1-101-93732-7 (lib. bdg.) | ISBN 978-1-101-93733-4 (ebook)
Subjects: | CYAC: Bedtime—Fiction. | Beds—Fiction. | Fear of the dark—Fiction. | Growth—Fiction.
Classification: LCC PZ8.3.B4595 My 2017 (print) | LCC PZ8.3.B4595 (ebook) |
DDC [E]—dc23

MANUFACTURED IN CHINA
10 9 8 7 6 5 4 3 2 1   First Edition

MY NEW BIG-KID BED

BY
DEBBIE BERTRAM

ILLUSTRATED BY
TAIA MORLEY

RANDOM HOUSE 🏠 NEW YORK

A birthday surprise from my mom
and my dad—
a new big-kid dinosaur bed!
A T. rex for me—
he's as cool as can be!
I'm excited to lay down my head!

"Is it my bedtime yet?
I can't wait to sleep."
Mom laughs.

"Sorry, not for a while.

It's quarter to four—just three hours more

until bedtime," she says with a smile.

After my dinner,
Dad gives me a bath.

Mom reads to me. I start to yawn.

When it's time
for "good night,"
they turn off
my light . . .

and after their kisses, they're gone.

The full moon is shining . . .
a shadow appears. . . .
Yikes! A dinosaur,
there on my wall!

It's scary and creepy, so now I'm not sleepy.
I run from my room, down the hall!

I poke my head in

to where my dog sleeps.

(I wish Mom had left on a light!)

I tug on old Rover—but he won't turn over!
No comfort from him, not tonight!

I run to the room where my grandma's asleep.

She's been here all week for a visit.

She lifts up her head from the comfortable bed

and whispers, "What's wrong, dear? What is it?"

"There's a BIG dinosaur on my wall,
and I'm SCARED!"

Grandma mumbles and just turns away.

She's tired and groggy.

Her words come out foggy....

I had hoped she'd invite me to stay!

I make a mad dash to
my mom and dad's room.
I can see that they're
both sound asleep.
I get into their bed,
avoiding Dad's head—
squeeze between them,
not making a peep.

It's crowded in here,
no room for a kid,
so I try hard
to make myself small.
I had hoped we could cuddle,
but now I just huddle—
my knees to my chest, in a ball.

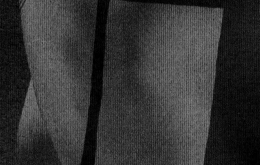

Mom's hogging the blankets,
and Dad has the pillows—
I try to grab on to the sheet.

Dad lets out a snore,
which is hard to ignore.
Then I feel something cold.
It's Mom's feet!

I crawl down between them, through blankets and sheets, getting out at the foot of their bed.

Tiptoe back to my room

with a feeling of doom.

I shiver from my toes to my head.

I peek into my bedroom . . .
I look all around.
Hey! That dinosaur's
not on my wall!

The moon's disappeared,

and the shadow I feared—

it's gone!

Now I'm not scared at all!

My new big-kid bed is waiting for me!

I am ready to start counting sheep....

In my very own bed, I lay down my head.

Yes! *This* is the best place to sleep!